ISBN: 1499298323 • ISBN:-13: 978-1499298321

Curly Bear

The Little Girl Bear
with the Curly, Curly Hair

Storyteller ❧ Jerry Kosel

Artist ❧ Anne Kosel

"It's really unfair,"
said the little girl bear,
"That I should have
such curly, curly hair."

"Other bears have
a nice smooth coat,
but my hair is so fuzzy,
I look like a goat."

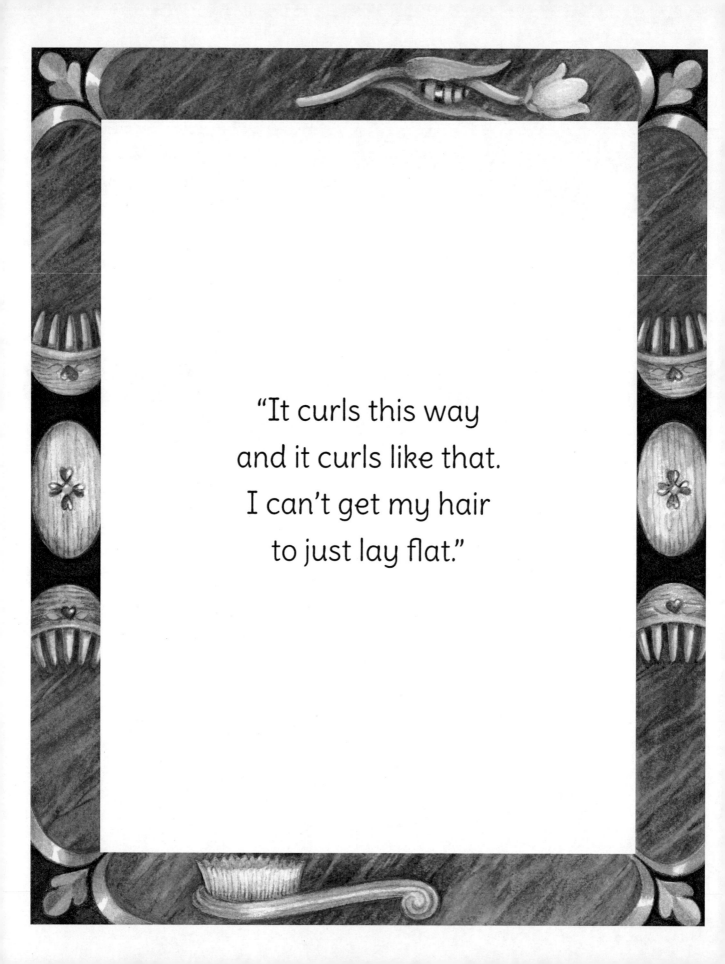

"It curls this way
and it curls like that.
I can't get my hair
to just lay flat."

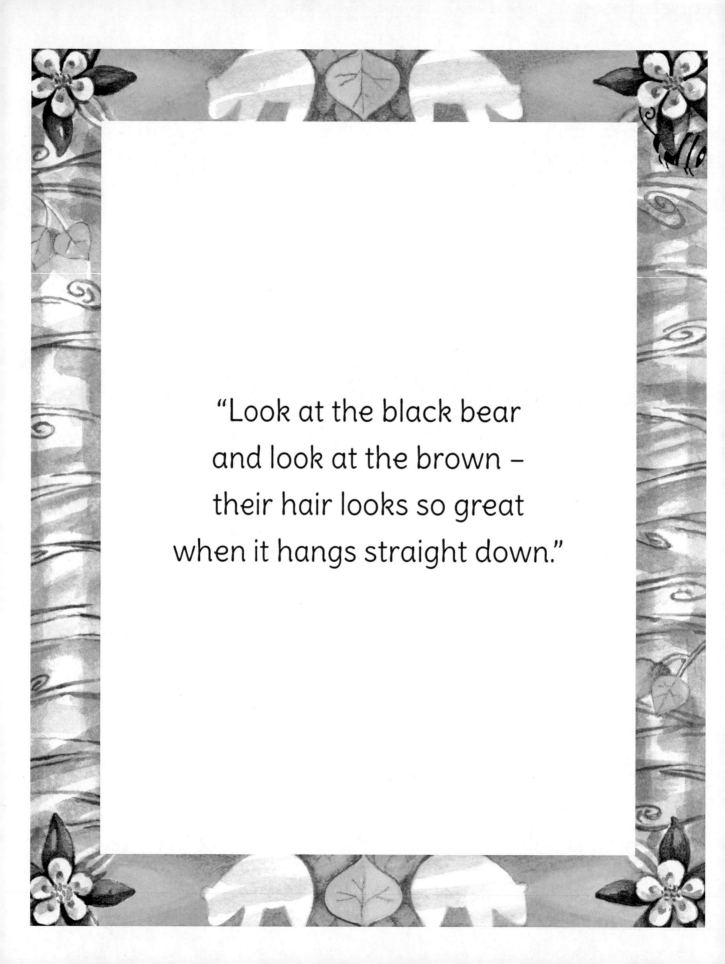

"Look at the black bear
and look at the brown –
their hair looks so great
when it hangs straight down."

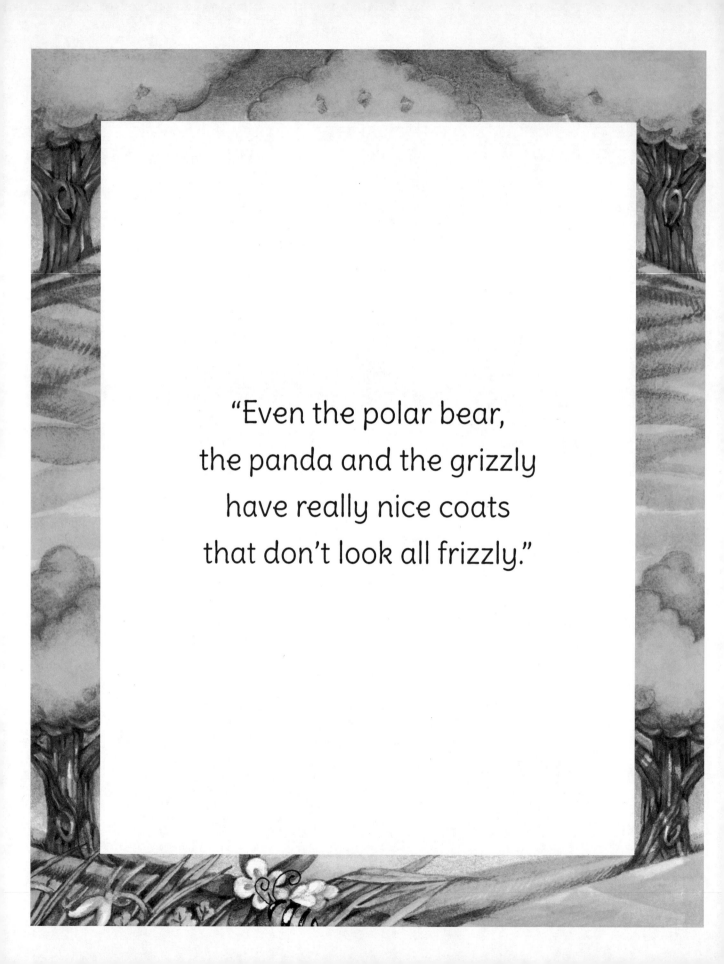

"Even the polar bear,
the panda and the grizzly
have really nice coats
that don't look all frizzly."

"Listen," said the mama
of the curly haired bear,
"You should be happy
to have hair so rare."

"Be glad for your hair,
you're an absolute doll!
If you were a pig,
you'd have no hair at all."

And the daddy bear added,
in a very deep voice,
"Listen to Mama,
for it's really your choice."

"Of all the bear cubs,
you have the prettiest curl.
Now give Daddy a hug,
my curly bear girl."

"Yeoow," yelled the little bear,
(she couldn't say "growl"),
"I'll spend the rest of my life
hiding under this towel."

"Mama doesn't love me.
My daddy doesn't care.
No one understands me,"
said the little curly bear.

Then Curly Bear went
to her bedroom to pout.
Outside of her window
she heard someone shout.

There on the lawn,
stood a little boy bear.
She was astonished to see,
he had curly, curly hair.

She ran out the door
and over by the tree,
and said to the boy bear,
"You look just like me."

"And you look like me,"
Cubby said with a smile.
"Wow, we're both really curly.
Want to play for a while?"

So they played for a while,
then went in and ate.
They didn't seem to care
if they were curly or straight.

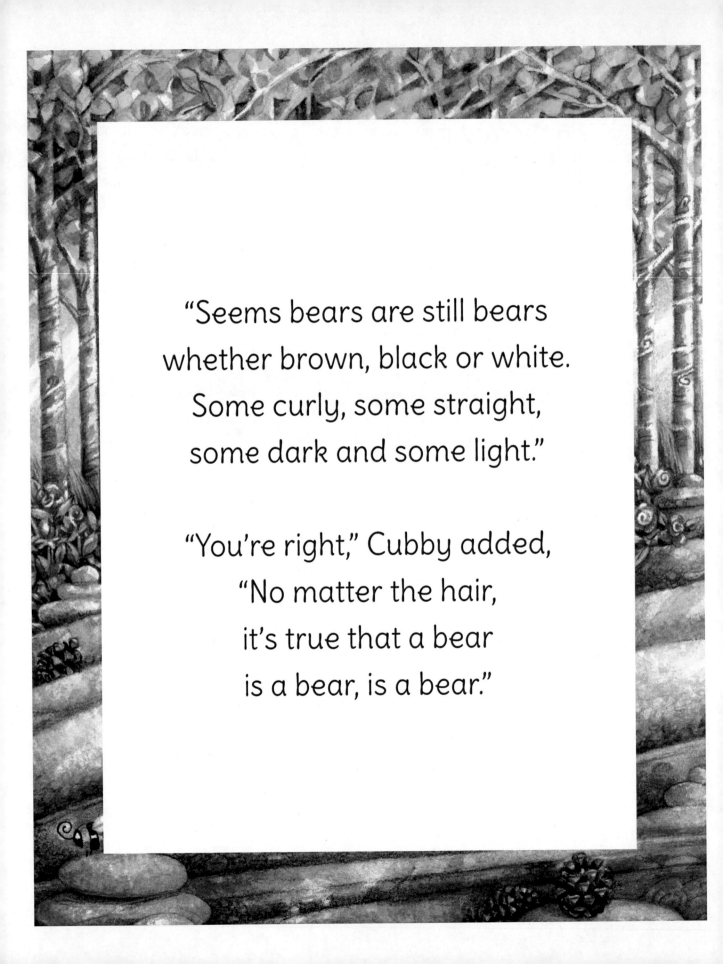

"Seems bears are still bears
whether brown, black or white.
Some curly, some straight,
some dark and some light."

"You're right," Cubby added,
"No matter the hair,
it's true that a bear
is a bear, is a bear."

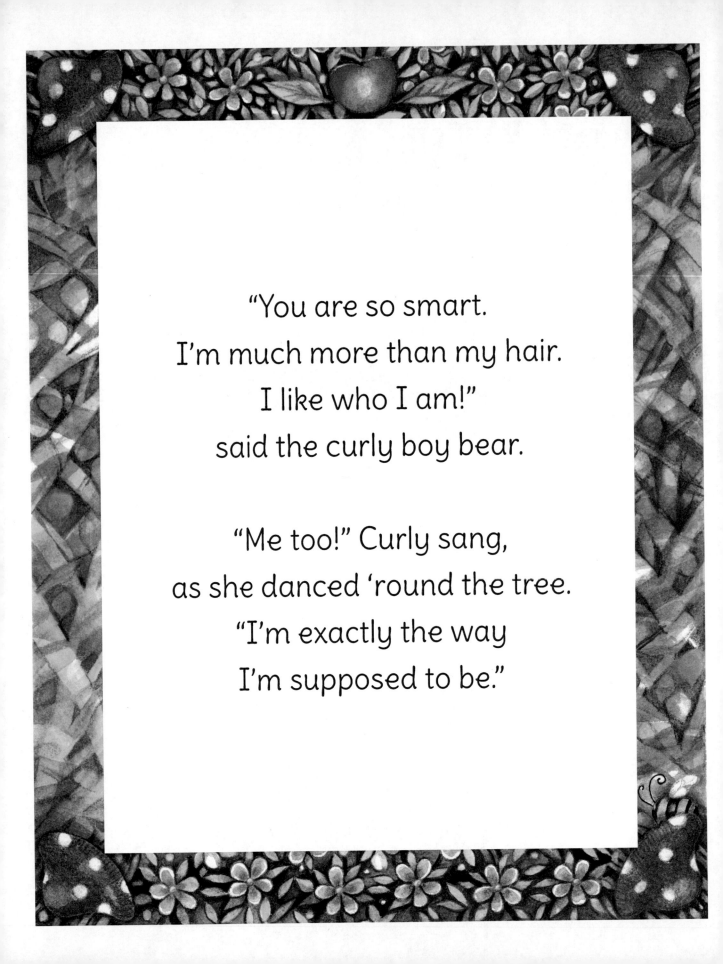

"You are so smart.
I'm much more than my hair.
I like who I am!"
said the curly boy bear.

"Me too!" Curly sang,
as she danced 'round the tree.
"I'm exactly the way
I'm supposed to be."

The End

Made in the USA
San Bernardino, CA
18 October 2016